SUPER RED
RIDING HOOD

For Yolanda, my super inspiration

Kids Can Press acknowledges the financial support of the Government of Ontario, through the Ontario Media Development Corporation's Ontario Book Initiative; the Ontario Arts Council; the Canada Council for the Arts; and the Government of Canada, through the CBF, for our publishing activity.

Published in Canada by
Kids Can Press Ltd.
25 Dockside Drive
Toronto, ON M5A 0B5

Published in the U.S. by
Kids Can Press Ltd.
2250 Military Road
Tonawanda, NY 14150

www.kidscanpress.com

The artwork in this book was rendered in Photoshop.
The text is set in Cloister URW.

Edited by Yasemin Uçar and Stacey Roderick
Designed by Claudia Dávila and Marie Bartholomew

This book is smyth sewn casebound.
Manufactured in Shenzhen, China, in 3/2014 through Asia Pacific Offset

CM 14 0 9 8 7 6 5 4 3 2 1

Library and Archives Canada Cataloguing in Publication

Dávila, Claudia, author, illustrator
   Super Red Riding Hood / Claudia Dávila.

ISBN 978-1-77138-020-1 (bound)

   I. Title.

PS8607.A95285S87 2014   jC813'.6   C2013-908162-3

Kids Can Press is a *corus*™ Entertainment company

SUPER RED RIDING HOOD

Claudia Dávila

Kids Can Press

NOT far from here, near a small forest, lives a girl named Ruby. Ruby's favorite color is red. She loves red berries, her red boots and especially the red cloak her grandma made for her. When Ruby puts on her red cloak, she becomes ...

SUPER RED RIDING HOOD!

One sunny afternoon, Ruby was very busy playing superhero in her room when she heard her mother call from downstairs.
"Ruby!"

"Is it something important, Mom?" she called back.
"It sure is!"
"Looks like Super Red Riding Hood has an important mission!" Ruby declared.

She threw on her red cloak and grabbed her flashlight. A superhero must be prepared for anything!

"You've been indoors all day," her mother said. "Why don't you go pick some raspberries to have with your snack?"

This did not sound like an important mission to Ruby, but she could see that her mom meant business.

Ruby kissed her mom goodbye and set out along the path to the raspberry bushes with her lunch box in hand.

"The woods are deep and dark and full of danger," Ruby said to herself. "But SUPER RED RIDING HOOD is never scared!"

Ruby was marching along bravely when,
OH, NO!
Ruby's big red rubber boot almost crushed
a tiny snail in the middle of the path!

"This is a dangerous place for
a little snail," she said. "Luckily,
SUPER RED RIDING HOOD
is here to rescue you!"

She carefully moved the little snail out of harm's way.

"A good deed done!" she said.

Ruby skipped toward the woods. *"Who's afraid of the deep dark woods, the deep dark woods, the deep dark woods? Who's afraid of the deep dark woods? Na na na, not me!"* she sang.

When she got to the edge of the forest, she stopped and peered ahead. A chill drifted out from the shadowy darkness.

"A superhero must be silent like a cat and watch out for danger," Ruby whispered, and tiptoed into the woods.

The forest was full of strange noises.
It was a very good thing she had
remembered to bring her flashlight.

HOO! HOO!

CRACK!

"Owl! Twig! Woodpecker!"
she said aloud, shining her bright
light toward the different sounds.

TACKA-
TACKA-
TACKA-
TACKA-
TACK!

"*Who's afraid of the deep dark woods,
the deep dark woods, the deep dark woods?
Who's afraid of the deep dark woods?
Na na na, not me!*" she sang as she walked.

Before long, she came to a sunny clearing, packed with raspberry bushes. She ran to fill her lunch box with juicy red berries.

"Mission accomplished!" she said triumphantly.

She was just snapping her lunch box closed, when she heard a new sound. A big, rumbly, growly, terrifying sound!

GRRRRRRR

Ruby's tummy twisted in a knot. Her teeth began to chatter.
A superhero must be brave, she reminded herself. *"Who's afraid
of the —"*

WOLF!!

He towered over Ruby, looking frightful with his sharp claws, his yellow fangs and his bushy tail swishing from side to side.

The wolf inched closer. Soon he was so close to
Ruby, she could feel his steamy breath on her face.
   "E-E-Excuse me, I'd like to get by," Ruby said,
in a smaller voice than she would have liked.
   The wolf didn't move.

He grinned and asked in a crackly growl, "Where are you going all alone in this big, dark forest?"

Ruby narrowed her eyes and peered at the shaggy beast.

"Why do you want to know?"

"Oh! Um ... just curious, I suppose. Maybe you can tell me this ..."

Before she could answer, the wolf lunged.
Quick as a rabbit, Super Red Riding Hood
hopped out of the way and used her super
skills to leap and dart past the tricky wolf.

ACK!!!

She scrambled up an oak tree and perched on a branch, just out of the wolf's reach. While she sat and caught her breath, the grumbly wolf skulked around the trunk of the tree.

Ruby had had enough. "Wolf,"
she called down, "let me pass!"
But the wolf stayed put.
"Wolf, I'm going to count to five.
You'd better leave me alone!"
The wolf still didn't move.

"One..." Ruby said firmly.

"Two..."

"Three..."

"FOUR..."

He could see that Ruby meant business.
"Okay, okay! I'll leave you alone."

Ruby started climbing back down the tree. But then ...

GRROWWLL

"WOLF?!"
"It ... It's my *tummy*," the wolf moaned.
"I'm just really hungry!"

"Well, why didn't you *say* so?"

Ruby jumped out of the tree, her red cloak floating down behind her like a parachute.

"If you wanted some of my snack, you could have just asked," she said.

The wolf looked at Ruby with a big, drooly smile. "Okay. Can I have some?" he asked, holding out a paw.

Ruby pulled her lunch box out of the wolf's reach. "Not so fast, Wolf! You really scared me before, snarling at me with your big fangs, and those sharp claws ..."

The wolf's ears drooped.
He looked at the ground.
"I'm sorry," he said.
    Ruby took a long look
at the sad, hungry wolf.

"Aw ... forget about it," she
said at last.
    The wolf perked up. "Please?"
he asked, very politely.

A superhero always helps those in need. So Super Red Riding Hood did what any superhero would do. She popped open her lunch box and shared the juicy berries.

As Ruby and the wolf snacked together under the big oak tree, Ruby remarked, "I didn't know wolves liked raspberries."

"Oh, yes," said the wolf cheerfully. "They're our favorite."

The wolf sat thinking for a little while as he munched.

"I didn't know little girls could be superheroes," he said.

"Oh, yes," said Ruby with a wide smile.
"We can."